PRENTICE-HALL, INC., Englewood Cliffs, N.J.

Hey, wait for me! I'm Amelia

Story and pictures by Linda Glovach

Hey, Wait For Me! I'm Amelia
by Linda Glovach

ISBN 0-13-387134-7
Library of Congress Catalog Card Number: 72-155492
Printed in the United States of America   *J*

Prentice-Hall International, Inc., London
Prentice-Hall of Australia, Pty. Ltd., Sydney
Prentice-Hall of Canada, Ltd., Toronto
Prentice-Hall of India Private Ltd., New Delhi
Prentice-Hall of Japan, Inc., Tokyo

ONE SATURDAY AMELIA HAD NOTHING IMPORTANT TO DO.

SHE COULD READ A BOOK

OR VISIT A FRIEND.

BUT INSTEAD,

SHE DECIDED TO TAKE A TRAIN

INTO THE CITY.

IN THE CITY

AMELIA WENT
TO A MUSEUM,

BOUGHT A BALLOON

AND SPENT SOME TIME IN THE PARK

DOING THINGS SHE LIKED TO DO.

LATER, AMELIA FELT HUNGRY

SO SHE HAD A HOT DOG

AND THEN

TOOK A WALK UPTOWN,

WHERE SHE BOUGHT A PRESENT FOR HER MOTHER

AND STOPPED TO WATCH
A GAME OF MARBLES.

BUT IT WAS GETTING LATE

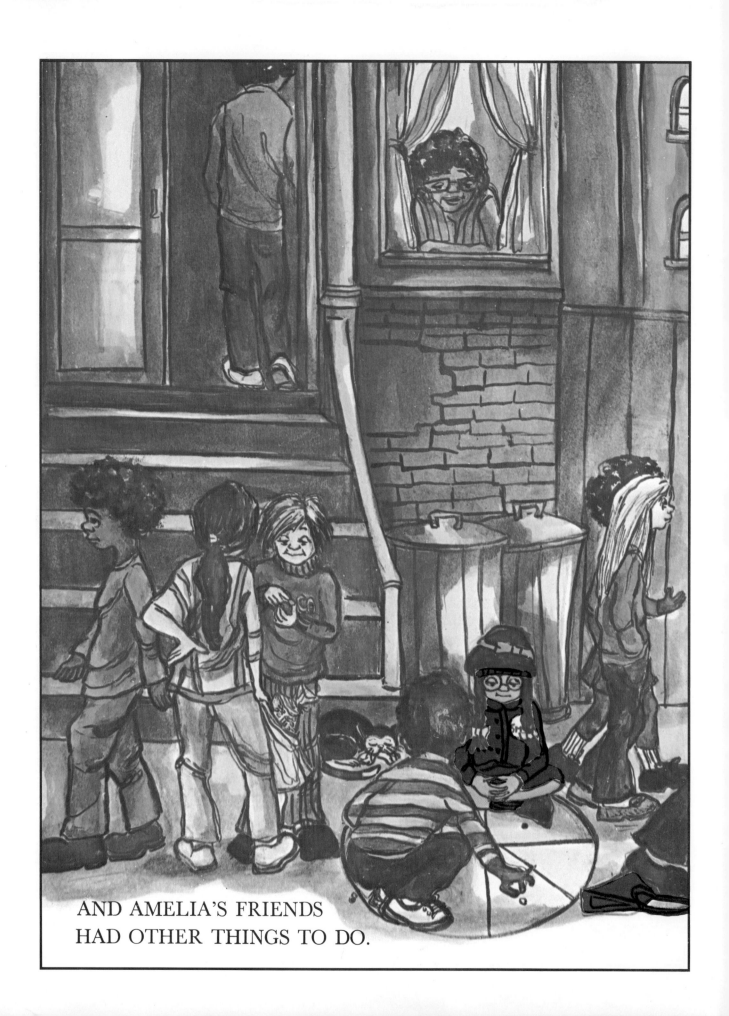

AND AMELIA'S FRIENDS
HAD OTHER THINGS TO DO.

SO SHE TOOK A BUS

BACK TO THE TRAIN STATION.

WHEN SHE GOT HOME
NO ONE KNEW SHE HAD GONE.